ZONDERKIDZ

VeggieTales Treasury
Copyright © 2012 by Big Idea, Inc. VEGGIETALES.® character names, likenesses and other
indicia are trademarks of Big Idea, Inc. All rights reserved.

Requests for information should be addressed to:
Zonderkidz, *Grand Rapids, Michigan 49530*

ISBN 978-0-310-60523-2

The Spoon in the Stone ISBN 9780310706267 (2005)
Field of Beans ISBN 9780310706281 (2005)
Lost in Place ISBN 9780310706298 (2005)
Cool Hand Cuke ISBN 9780310707387 (2006)
Snooze Brothers ISBN 9780310707394 (2006)
Frog Wars ISBN 9780310706274 (2005)
Ben Hurry ISBN 9780310707431 (2006)
West Side Story ISBN 9780310707424 (2006)

Any Internet addresses (websites, blogs, etc.) and telephone numbers printed in this book
are offered as a resource. They are not intended in any way to be or imply an endorsement
by Zondervan, nor does Zondervan vouch for the content of these sites and numbers for
the life of this book.

Written by: Doug Peterson
Illustrated by: Michael Moore
Original editor: Cindy Kenney
Editor: Mary Hassinger
Original art direction and design: Karen Poth
Cover design: Cindy Davis

Printed in China

12 13 14 15 16 /LPC/ 10 9 8 7 6 5 4 3 2 1

"Anyone who wants to be important among you must be your servant."

(Mark 10:43)

The Spoon in the Stone

By Doug Peterson
Illustrated by Michael Moore

bigidea.com

ZONDERVAN.com/
AUTHORTRACKER
follow your favorite authors

"Run, Junior, run!"

shouted Laura Carrot. "Leave the soccer ball behind!"

Junior Asparagus tore across Mr. Picklesheimer's backyard. Right behind him was a dog with ferocious fangs. The beast snarled and snapped.

Mr. Picklesheimer didn't like kids on his lawn so he bought a dog. Correction. He bought a creature that was part monster.

Junior ran for his life!

Just as the dog was about to attack, Junior leaped over the fence. He was safe. But the soccer ball didn't make it. The dog tore it to pieces and gobbled it up.

Junior gulped. That soccer ball could have been him!

The Next Day...

Junior's mom told him that everyone was going to help Mr. Picklesheimer!
"What?" exclaimed Junior.

"Mr. Picklesheimer is getting old, and he needs help doing his yard work.
So our family and the Carrots are going to help him. God wants us to serve
others, Junior."

"Today?" Junior gasped. "Laura and I have more important things to do!"

"There's nothing more important than serving others," Mr. Asparagus said. "We need you home by one o'clock."

Junior sighed. He didn't like this—**AT ALL**.

Later That Morning...

Junior and Laura complained loudly in the Treasure Trove Bookstore in the heart of VeggieTown.

"Why should we help a grouchy old pickle?" Laura muttered. "We have more important things to do."

Mr. O'Malley couldn't help but overhear. "Aye, you're having the same problem a lad and lassie had in a storybook I once read. Let's see if I can find it," said the Irish potato who owned the store.

"It's somewhere in the *Serving Others* section, right next to the Scratch-and-Sniff Classics," he mumbled. "Ahhh, here it is. It's called *The Spoon in the Stone*."

Junior opened to the first page and saw a huge castle with a draw-bridge. Standing in front of the castle were two Veggies in royal clothes.

Four words lifted up from the page into the air! They swirled around and around, growing larger and larger! Four simple words:

ONCE UPON A TIME.

All At Once...

   The four giant words swirled around Junior and Laura and...
WHOOOOOOOOOOOOOOOSHHHH!
Junior and Laura found themselves falling
down
   down
      down.
   Everything was a blur as they zoomed straight through piles of
large words...and landed right in front of the castle door.

"Welcome to Hamalot!" shouted the tomato. "I'm Sir Irving, and this is my assistant, Sir Galaham. We run the Hamalot Hotel!"

"We like ham. **A LOT**," grinned the cucumber.

"We've been expecting you," said Sir Irving.

Junior and Laura blinked in surprise. "Huh?"

"Here's your apron," said Sir Galaham, "and your tray."

"Don't dilly-dally!" urged Sir Irving. "The hotel is packed with giants and ogres for this weekend's FE-FI-FO-FUN Trade Show. We have a shortage of servants!"

Irving and Galaham hurried them across a drawbridge. "There's much to do," Irving explained. "The Hamalot is the only place that leaves a ham on your pillow every evening instead of a mint."

Galaham grinned. "We like ham. **A LOT**."

"You can start on tables and deliver room service," explained Irving. He took Junior and Laura into the Hamalot Restaurant, which specialized in ham and beans, peanut butter and ham sandwiches, and banana-ham smoothies.

"You really do like ham. **A LOT**," observed Junior.

The restaurant was piled high with dirty dishes. Three lazy knights gobbled up food and played ping-pong with a hamball.

"That's Sir Nezzer, Sir Phillipe, and Sir Luntalot. They used to be hotel servants, but after they became knights, they decided they were too important to help around the hotel."

"These lazy knights used to be known as the Knights of the Round Table. But with no servants to clean up, the Round Table piled up with dirty dishes. So they switched tables and became the Knights of the Pool Table. Then they became the Knights of the Card Table. Now they're the Knights of the Ping-Pong Table," said Irving.

At That Very Second...

A pea ran up to Sir Irving and handed him a slip of paper.

"Here's your first job!" Irving said. "We've got a rush order of ham and bean soup. Deliver it to Room 53!"

The Knights of the Ping-Pong Table suddenly stopped playing. The hamball bounced off of the table and clunked Sir Nezzer in the helmet. It knocked his visor shut, on his tongue.

"Outh."

"Room 53?" gasped Sir Phillipe. "That's the dreaded giant Grizzle's room."

"Grizzle is in the Deluxe Dungeon Suite," noted Sir Luntalot. "And he's very dangerous."

"Thath right," said Sir Nezzer, whose tongue was still caught.

Junior and Laura looked at each other. "Maybe we'd better not bother him."

"Nonsense," said Sir Irving as he handed the tray of food to Junior. "You'll be fine! Besides, if you don't serve him this food, Grizzle will tear apart our hotel."

A Little While Later...

Laura knocked on the door to Room 53, and a giant pickle swung open the door. "WHAT TOOK YOU SO LONG?" he boomed.

If Junior had knees, they would've been shaking. A large dragon lurked behind the giant. Steam curled from its nose, which set off the smoke alarm.

The giant pickle roared and smashed the alarm into bits.

Junior cleared his throat and tried to be brave. "Your soup, sir."

The giant stared down at the bowl. "DA SPOON! WHERE'S DA SPOON?"

They forgot the spoon!

"I'll get it," Laura volunteered.

"*You* stay with *me*!" the giant roared. "If da little asparagus can't find da spoon before da Hamalot tower bell rings, den I'll have carrot stew instead."

Junior dashed back to the kitchen. All the spoons were caked solid with gunk!

"Please help me find a clean spoon!" Junior begged the Knights of the Ping-Pong Table.

"Sorry, we're knights, not servants," said Sir Luntalot.

"But God wants us to serve others!" Junior begged.

"Sorry," said Sir Nezzer. "We've got better things to do—like playing ping-pong."

Junior spotted a large spoon sticking out from a huge rock in the courtyard. He ran up to the spoon and grabbed the handle as the others gathered around him to see what would happen.

"That spoon is stuck in ancient oatmeal," explained Sir Galaham. "Many knights have tried to pull it out. But no one can do it."

Junior gave a mighty yank. The spoon wouldn't budge.

Then it happened. Junior gave a final tug, and the spoon slid from the stone, as smooth as butter. Trumpets sounded. Sunlight broke through the clouds. Everyone cheered!

Holding the spoon high like a sword, Junior dashed back into the hotel. But he was too late. The Hamalot tower bell was ringing.

After sprinting upstairs to Grizzle's room, Junior swung open the door. Was he too late to save his friend?

He held his breath...

"Oh hi, Junior!" chirped Laura. "Mr. Grizzle and I are having tea."

"Huh?"

"After I gave Mr. Grizzle some tea, he calmed down," Laura continued. "He's really quite friendly."

Junior held out the golden spoon. "Your spoon, Mr. Grizzle."

Grizzle's eyes widened. "It's da *famous* spoon in da stone!"

"They say whoever pulls the spoon from the stone has a true servant's heart," Galaham explained.

"God wants us to be a servant to others," Junior smiled.

Later, in the courtyard, Sir Galaham asked Junior and Laura to kneel before him.

"I dub thee Sir Junior and Lady Laura," he said, gently tapping them on the head with the spoon.

"Hold it!" shouted Sir Phillipe. "By making them a knight and a lady, they'll be too important to be our servants!"

"Don't worry," Junior told them.

"There's nothing more important than serving others," Laura added. "Even when you're a knight."

Sir Galaham grinned. "I like that. **A LOT**."

Just Then...

"Uh-oh," said Grizzle. "I think you're at **DA END** of da story."

"We'll miss you," Junior called.

In a Blink...

They were back in the Treasure Trove Bookstore.

"Well, how did you like the book?" asked Mr. O'Malley, shuffling over to them with sandwiches and pink lemonade. "Learn anything about serving others?"

Junior and Laura stared at the old irish potato, still stunned by their adventure.

"Do **ALL** of your books do this?" Junior asked.

"Do what, laddie?" Mr. O'Malley asked as he set down the tray.

"You know. Pull you into the story?"

"Ahhh, all good stories pull you in," the potato said with a wink. "Here. Have a ham sandwich."

"Thanks," said Laura. "But we gotta get back home."

"Ahhh! That's right," agreed Mr. O'Malley. "You've got to help a neighbor, don't ya, lassie? But I thought you had more important things to do?"

Junior and Laura looked at each other.

"Nah," said Junior. "We can play later."

"Aye, that's the spirit!"

Mr. O'Malley watched as Junior and Laura dashed out the door. Then he sighed, took a big bite of ham sandwich, and smiled.

I sure like ham, he said to himself. **A LOT.**

In short, there's simply not
A more amazing spot
For happily serving other folks
Like a place called HAM-A-LOT!

Elijah went there and stood in front of the people.
He said, "How long will it take you to make up your minds?
If the Lord is the one and only God, follow him."

(1 Kings 18:21)

Field of Beans

By Doug Peterson
Illustrated by Michael Moore

bigidea.com

ZONDERVAN.com/
AUTHORTRACKER
follow your favorite authors

The bases were loaded in the last inning. Two outs.

Junior Asparagus stood at the plate with three balls and two strikes.

If Junior smacked a base hit, he would knock in the winning runs.

Lenny Carrot pitched the ball, everything seemed to move in slow motion. The fans held their breath.

Junior swung.

"Steeeeerike three!" yelled the umpire. The Mighty Junior struck out.

Back in the Dugout...

"Nice going, Asparagus. You lost us the game," grumbled Boog Pickle, the meanest kid on Junior's team. "If you carried a rabbit's foot for good luck, you wouldn't strike out."

"Everyone has something for good luck—except you," added Percy Pea.

It was true. Laura Carrot carried a lucky horseshoe. Boog Pickle tapped the bench three times with his bat every inning. And Jimmy and Jerry Gourd didn't wash their uniforms when the team was on a winning streak.

Judging by their smell, the team had been winning—a lot. Until today.

Junior didn't carry good luck charms because he didn't believe they had special powers. But now he wasn't so sure.

"Just because everyone else is doing something, doesn't make it right," said Reverend Archibald, the coach of Junior's team. "God wants us to follow him, not the crowd. He'll always lead us in the right direction."

Junior sighed.

"A lucky rabbit's foot can't change how a game turns out," Reverend Archibald added.

"I just don't know anymore," Junior muttered.

Later That Afternoon...

Junior wandered into the Treasure Trove Bookstore. "Mr. O'Malley, you're Irish," Junior said to the bookstore owner. "Do you have any lucky four-leaf clovers?"

"I'm afraid I don't, laddie," grinned the potato. "But I do have a storybook you might like to read."

Mr. O'Malley dug through a shelf, yanking out books left and right. "The book is somewhere in the *Sticking-Up-for-What-You-Believe-In* section, right next to the Pop-up Math Books."

"Ahhh, here's the one. It's called *Field of Beans*." When Junior opened the first page, he saw a huge stadium packed with thousands of baseball fans.

At That Very Moment...

Four giant words floated up from the stands of the stadium. Four simple words: ONCE UPON A TIME.

Suddenly...

The four words swirled around Junior. They whirled and twirled and
WHOOOOOOOOOOSH!
Junior tumbled over
and over
and over.

He somersaulted through the stands...and landed right in the stadium.

"You're just in time, Coach!" said a funny-looking grape, running up to Junior.

Junior was baffled. "Why did you call me Coach?"

"Because you're my coach. Coach!" said the grape "My name is Eli, and this is the biggest game of the year!"

The stadium was packed with screaming, chanting fans.

"Everyone is rooting for the other team, but that's okay," said Eli. "I don't mind going against the crowd when they're rooting for the Relics."

"Who are the Relics?" Junior asked.

"You don't know who the Baal City Relics are?" Eli exclaimed. "The Relics have won the championship for the last forty years."

Eli explained that everyone wanted to play for the Relics because they had such a great record.

"Why do the Relics keep winning so much?" asked Junior.

"Well, if you ask *them*, they will tell you it's because of the idols they worship," Eli explained.

"They worship idols?" Junior asked. "What kind of idols?"

"Lucky idols," said Eli. "You see that bean over there? His name is Shoehorn Joe. He's a legend. He wears that little gold-plated shoehorn in every game because he thinks it will make him win."

"Why don't YOU start wearing a lucky charm like the Relics?" Junior asked.

"I don't believe in 'em," Eli said. "I follow the Lord, the only one, true God. I don't trust in lucky charms, I trust in God. And today's the big showdown between the Relics and the Lord."

The crowd roared, as hundreds of beans ran out on the field. They jumped up and down and tackled each other. They really knocked themselves out.

"Is that THE TEAM?" Junior asked. He was a little worried about the odds.

"Yep, those are the players for Baal City. All 450 of them. You sure don't know much about this game, do ya kid. Tell you what. Try listening to the announcers. They'll tell you what's happening in the game."

He motioned toward a nearby booth where a tomato and a cucumber were hunched behind their microphones.

"Welcome to the match-up of the century!" said one announcer. "My name is Bob the Tomato."

"...and I'm Larry the Cucumber. It's a beautiful day for a Baal game. Not a cloud in the sky!"

"Uh, Larry...It hasn't rained for three years," noted Bob. "A cloud in the sky would be nice."

"Oh, right. Drat," said Larry. "But have we got a game for you! It's the Mount Carmel Dodgers versus the Baal City Relics. **Let's get ready to rumble!**"

"Tell us a little about today's game, Larry," said Bob.

"Sure thing, Bobbo. Both teams are going to wheel out a HUGE barbeque grill and pile it high with their favorite ballpark snacks. The Relics are going to rely on their lucky idols to get their charcoal started. And Eli is going to ask the Lord to start his grill. Whoever gets their grill lit first–wins! Not to mention they get a whole bunch of delicious hot dogs and nachos with melty, bubbly, warm cheese on top."

The game kicked off with Baal City. The Relics rolled their grill out into the middle of the field. Then players bowed before the grill and began rubbing their lucky charms and praying to their idols.

"Answer us!" they shouted.

No answer.

"Come on, idol, light our fire!" they yelled.

No fire.

"Please! Just a spark!"

No spark.

One Half Hour Later...

"It looks like the Baal City Relics are in big trouble, Larry," Bob reported. "They're calling up players from their bullpen."

Larry wasn't paying attention. He was too busy standing up and singing.

"Take me out to the Baal Game. Take me out to the crowd.
Buy me some peanuts and matzo dough. Follow God! It's the best way to go.
So it's root, root, root for our Lord's team! If you do, you'll be glad that you came!
Cuz it's one! Two! Three strikes you're out! At the old Baal Game!"

Larry was right. The Baal City Relics were striking out. They still couldn't get
a fire to light in their grill.

Many, Many Hours Later...

No matter how hard the Relics rubbed their lucky charms and prayed to their idols, their grill wouldn't start. Shoehorn Joe rubbed the gold plating right off his shoehorn, but still the fire wouldn't start.

It was finally the Dodgers' turn.

"What can you tell us about the Dodgers, Larry?" asked Bob.

"Well, Bobbo, they only have one player on their team, but he's an all-star," said Larry. "His name is Eli, and he's good at dodging trouble from the League Commissioner. With a lifetime average of 356, he leads the league in the wilderness."

"No wonder he was named most valuable player two years in a row!" noted Bob.

"That's right, Bobbo," said Larry. "He was in the minors for two seasons, but he worked his way up to being a Major Prophet in record time."

"He's being coached by a little asparagus," Bob said. "But what's this?" Bob said. "I can't believe it, Larry!"

Eli soaked the grill with kiwi, watermelon, and grape juice three separate times. Coach Junior had a fit.

"What are you doing?" Junior yelled. "The charcoal's not going to burn if you dump juice on it! Use lighter fluid!"

"The Lord can start this grill on fire, even when it's soaked with juice," Eli explained. "He can do anything!"

Junior just shook his head.

Then Eli stepped forward and boldly began to pray.

"Lord, you are the God of Abraham, Isaac, and Israel. Let everyone know that you are God in Baal City. Answer me, Lord. Then these people will know that you are the one and only God."

The crowd went so quiet that you could hear a mosquito sneeze.

"Achoo!"

"God bless you," whispered Larry.

And then it happened...

A brilliant bolt of lightning blasted the grill, sending the hot dogs and pretzels toward the hungry fans.

The crowd roared.

"That grill is outta here!" shouted Bob.

"And the fans are going crazy!" yelled Larry. "With God's help, Eli stood up against the crowd and pulled off an amazing victory! That's one for the Book!"

After a Long Celebration...

Two words suddenly appeared on the scoreboard. Two simple words:

THE END.

Junior knew what that meant. The story was over.

"You were incredible," Junior said to Eli.

"Not me Junior, the Lord. Just remember to follow God and not the crowd. He will do incredible things in your life, too."

All at Once...

Junior felt himself being pulled toward the scoreboard. Closer and closer and...

The next thing he knew, Junior found himself back in the Treasure Trove Bookstore. The roaring crowd was still ringing in his ears.

The Next Day...

Junior stepped up to bat. Once again, Boog Pickle blocked his way.

"I hope you got a lucky charm," snarled Boog.

"Sorry, Boog," Junior said. "Lucky charms don't have any power."

"If good luck charms don't have power, then how did Laura Carrot just get a big hit?"

Laura hurried from first base over to second. But then she slowed down.

"Hey! What's wrong with her?" Boog muttered.

"Yer out!" yelled the umpire as Laura looked back to see the horseshoes fall from her pocket.

"These goofy things slowed me down," she complained. "They weigh a ton! I'm not carrying them around any more. Lucky charms don't really work, anyway."

From That Day On...

Boog didn't bother Junior again.

Sometimes Junior got hits. Sometimes he didn't. Sometimes his team won. Sometimes they didn't. But Junior always followed God both on and off the field. As for Mr. O'Malley, he was always in the stands, singing this song:

Take me out to the Baal Game. Take me out to the crowd.
Buy me some peanuts and matzo dough. Follow God! It's the best way to go.
So it's root, root, root for our Lord's team! If you do, you'll be glad that you came!
Cuz it's one! Two! Three strikes you're out! At the old Baal Game!

"So do not be afraid. I am with you. Do not be terrified.
I am your God. I will make you strong and help you."

(Isaiah 41:10)

Lost In Place

By Cindy Kenney
Illustrated by Michael Moore

bigidea.com

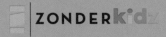

ZONDERVAN.com/
AUTHORTRACKER
follow your favorite authors

"Junior! Come out, come out wherever you are!" Laura called.

"You'll never find me!" Junior Asparagus giggled as he darted down an alley and ran out onto a sidewalk. He dove behind some bushes and snuggled into a hiding spot.

After a few minutes, Junior peeked around the bushes. No sign of Laura. In fact, there was no sign of anything familiar. Where was he?

The sun began to set and darkness crept in. Still no sign of Laura.

Junior slipped out from behind the bushes. He looked to his left, then to his right. He didn't know the way home!

Meanwhile, Back at the Asparagus House...

Laura described to Junior's mom and dad what happened.

"I called and called his name. But he never came out!" she cried.

Junior's mom and dad looked at each other. Where could Junior be?

In the Meantime...

Junior tried to find his way home. He didn't recognize anything or anyone. Turning a corner, he headed down a dark alley. Was it just his imagination, or was something watching him?

As Junior neared the end of the alley, a large, square shadow with heavy footsteps approached.

"*Footsteps*?" Junior mumbled. "In *VeggieTown*?"

Startled by the sound, Junior turned and ran the opposite direction. At the other end of the alley, two large shadows moved toward him. Junior heard heavy breathing. He choked back a tear.

"Junior!" called one of the figures.

How do they know my name? he thought.

"Junior! Where are you?" called the other voice.

It was his mom and dad!

"Boy, am I glad to see you guys! I was really scared!" Junior confessed. "A big monster was chasing after me!"

"Do you mean this nice police officer?" asked Junior's mom.

Junior turned around to see an officer smiling down at him.

"We were worried too, Junior," said his dad. He was out of breath after running all over VeggieTown. "But God watches over you. He's with you wherever you go."

"If you put your trust in God, he will make you strong and help you through anything you're afraid of," added his mom.

Junior was glad to hear that. But he just wanted to go home.

The Next Day...

Junior refused to leave the house. Percy Pea asked him to go to the park. Laura Carrot asked him to ride bikes. His mom and dad encouraged him to go over to a friend's house. But Junior was too afraid to go anywhere.

"Let's go to the Treasure Trove Bookstore," Junior's mom suggested. "You can pick out a good book to read if you're going to stay home all day."

At the Bookstore...

Mrs. Asparagus told Mr. O'Malley that Junior got lost. She asked him to help them find a good adventure to read.

"Aye! It just so happens I have a story that takes place in outer space. Let's see...where is it now?" The Irish Potato shuffled through some of the books and said, "Here we go. It's right between the *Using Your Noodle When You Doodle* books and *God Is Bigger Than the Boogie Man*. It's called *Lost in Place*. Take a look at it, lad."

Inside the storybook Junior saw a spaceship flying through a galaxy filled with stars and planets.

At That Very Moment...

    Four words lifted up from the galaxy and swirled around Junior. Four little words tumbling a
twirling through shooting stars: **ONCE UPON A TIME**.

All at Once...

WHOOOOOOOOOOOOOSSSHHHHH! Junior was caught up in the stars and went

racing,
  tumbling,
    twirling,

and landed right inside a spaceship.

"The ship's new crew member is here!" Don Quest called out to the Rattleson family. "Welcome to the Jitterbug 2!"

"Huh?" asked Junior, nervously looking around. Once again, he found himself in unfamiliar territory.

"What happened to the Jitterbug 1?" Junior asked.

"That bug lost its jitter in a meteor storm last year. But I got this ship up and running in no time, and we're back on course. This ship can jitterbug, do the watoosie, and dance a pretty mean Hokey Pokey."

A gourd with squinty eyes turned away from his telescope so he could analyze Junior. "What kind of experience do you have?"

"Umm..." blinked Junior.

"That's Dr. Smirk, our ship's scientist," Mr. Rattleson explained. "But his way of doing things is a little different, if you ask me," he whispered. "The Rattleson family is on their way to find a new home in the Alphabeta Solar System."

"But we can't find our way," Dr. Smirk sneered.

"We keep getting lost," added Mr. Rattleson as he checked several instruments on the Jitterbug 2.

"Lost-is-an-ac-cu-rate-an-swer," beeped a robot. "Dr.-Smirk's-dir-ec-tion-form-u-las-are-in-cor-rect."

"We didn't ask for your opinion, robot," barked Dr. Smirk.

"How do ya do," Pa Rattleson said, changing the subject. "We're the Rattleson family. This here's the rest of the clan—Ma, Penny, Will, and Judy."

"Howdy!" said Ma.

"Kin he help us find our way through this here solar system, Pa?" asked Will.

"Me?" Junior asked, surprised.

Just Then...

The ship began to jitter.

"Hang on, everybody!" called Ma Rattleson.

"How do we do that, Ma?" asked Judy, looking down at her sides.

The ship veered to the left and everyone tipped left. The ship veered to the right, and everyone rolled back to the right. Then the ship bobbled up and down.

"It's a meteor shower!" Don yelled.

Everyone grabbed a shower cap and ran frantically around the ship.

"I'll git some shampoo!"

"I'll git the fresh towels!"

"I'll git an umbrella!"

"Git outta my way, you frazzled, frizzle brain!" Will grumbled.

"You git outta my way, you jittery-jumping bean!" Penny griped in return.

"Stop yer fightin'! We're in a crisis!" yelled Ma Rattleson.

The Jitterbug 2 crew bumped this way and that, causing more problems than helping.

Then came the dreaded words...

"We're off course! We've lost our place in space—again!"
Everyone stopped. They stared at the robot as he confirmed the announcement.
"Oh no!" gulped Junior. He knew his mom and dad wouldn't be able to save him this time!
"Ahhhhhhhhhhhhh!" screamed the Rattlesons.

When Suddenly...

They heard someone yell, "STOP!"

"Umm...er...we probably shouldn't panic," Junior suggested as he took a big gulp of air.

Everyone stopped to stare at Junior. With all eyes focused on him, Junior wondered how he could help the crew of the Jitterbug 2.

"Have you ever thought that we're not alone in all this?" Junior asked.

"Nope," said Will.

"Not me," said Judy.

"Not a chance," agreed Penny.

Junior realized he felt alone, just like the others. Then said to himself,
God watches over you. He is with you wherever you go.

"Hey everybody! God is watching over us, right now," Junior began. "He never leaves us...even when we're in a different solar system!"

Then Junior remembered his mom's words, too.

If you put your trust in God, he will make you strong and help you through anything you're afraid of.

"And God wants us to trust him so he can help us find our way through anything. If we remember that, we can all figure out what to do."

Everyone blinked and looked at each other. Could this be true?

Finally...

Don Quest decided to speak. "I just followed Dr. Smirk's orders!"

"Is that true?" Pa demanded.

Dr. Smirk turned away. "I didn't want to mislead you. But I heard the Alphabeta Solar System only liked Veggies who know their ABC's," he explained. "I don't know mine, so I was afraid no one would like me."

"So you gave us bad directions?" gasped Judy.

"You went and got us lost on purpose?" asked Will.

"Dr. Smirk, you don't have to be afraid either," Junior said. "No matter where you go, you're never alone because God is with you. It doesn't matter if you're lost, or if you find yourself in a new situation. God will help you through anything."

"That-mes-sage-com-putes," agreed the robot. "'Do-not-be-a-fraid. I-am-with-you. Do-not-be-ter-ri-fied. I-am-your-God. I-will-make-you-strong-and-help-you.' Isaiah-41:10."

Don Quest buckled himself back in and turned the ship around, confident that God was watching over them.

Ma and Pa turned back to the controls. "We need some help cleaning the shampoo off these levers!"

"That ain't gonna be a problem, Ma. God kin help us git through anything!" said Will.

"And I can help Dr. Smirk with his ABC's." said Penny.

Dr. Smirk thanked Penny and started to work on a new formula. Knowing God was with him, he trusted he would find a new way to get to the Alphabeta Solar System. So he inserted a new direction formula into the robot.

"Dr.-Smirk's-cal-cu-la-tions-are-cor-rect," confirmed the robot. "We-are-back-on-course."

Everyone cheered.

As the ship headed into the Alphabeta Solar System, several letters swirled into view: **THE END.** Junior waved good-bye as he was pulled back through space.

In a Twinkling...

Junior found himself back inside the Treasure Trove Bookstore.

"*Lost in Place*?" asked Mrs. Asparagus. "Mr. O'Malley, do you have anything else? I don't think Junior wants to read about getting lost."

"That's okay, Mom. I'm never alone because God is with me!" Junior told her.

"Aye, lad! That's true," Mr. O'Malley said with a wink.

Just then, the little bell above the Treasure Trove Bookstore's door began to twinkle. The family that entered looked just like the Rattleson family from the Jitterbug 2!

"Excuse us," said the older grape. "I think we're lost. We sure could use some directions."
"Aye, I'd be happy to help, sir," Mr. O'Malley said. "What are you looking for?"
"Planet Earth."
Junior couldn't hide his surprise.
"Well, then there's no need to fear," Mr. O'Malley answered. "You've already found it!"

"Hands that don't want to work make you poor.
But hands that work hard bring wealth to you."

(Proverbs 10:4)

Cool Hand Cuke

By Cindy Kenney
Illustrated by Michael Moore

bigidea.com

ZONDERVAN.com/
AUTHORTRACKER
follow your favorite authors

"Let's all do the hop, Oh Baby, let's all do the hop."
Jimmy and Jerry sang as they entered the Veggie-HOP café. Junior and
Laura were busy working to raise money for the VeggieTown Hospital.

"Junior!" shouted Laura. "Customers!"

Junior rolled his eyes. He dragged himself away from his peanut-butter milk shake and seated Jimmy and Jerry.

Laura took an order at another table.

"Do you have zee French fries?" asked Jean Claude.

"Or zee French toast?" asked Phillipe.

"No," Laura explained. "Everything we serve at the House of Peanut Butter has peanut butter in it."

"Order up!" called the cook.

Laura spotted Junior sitting with Jimmy and Jerry. "Junior! Please get that order!"

"We're not raising much money," Junior moaned.

"C'mon Junior, please!" Laura begged. "It will be worth it, you'll see."

"It's not worth it. I'm wasting my whole summer vacation and I won't have a thing to show for it," Junior grumbled as he jumped out of the booth.

He didn't see Laura, who was carrying a tray full of peanut-butter fritters.

CRASH!

"That's it. I quit," Junior said and stomped out the door.

That evening Junior wandered into the Treasure Trove Bookstore.
"What's got your feathers all ruffled, lad?" Mr. O'Malley asked.
"I don't want to work during summer vacation if I don't get to keep the money" Junior said.

"Looking to get rich, are ya?" the Irish potato said with a wink.
Wham! A big book plopped down in front of Junior.
"A vacation book?" Junior asked.
"Better than that. It's a trip to a farm where you'll find real wealth."
Junior read the title, "Cool Hand Cuke."

As he opened the book, the words "Once Upon A Time" began to swirl around and . . .

WHOOOOOOOOOOOOSH!

Junior found himself racing **down**
down
down
right into the middle of a farm.

"Ah! The new farmhand," a tomato said.

"I'm Hot Hand Tomato," he said. "This is my partner, Cool Hand Cuke."
He shoved a basket at Junior and said, "We've got lots of work to do before sundown. You can help us finish up in the barn."

"This is supposed to be my vacation," whined Junior.

In the barn they were greeted by a grape with mirrored sunglasses.
"If you fill your baskets before sundown, you get a prize from the box,"
barked the grape. "If you feed the chickens by ten, you get a prize from the
box. Sweep the barn by noon, and you get a prize from the box."

Junior glanced at the prize box. It contained lots of stuff like a yo-yo, tennis shoes, and a sombrero, but not riches.

"Finishin' up over here, boss," said Cool Hand Cuke. He showed him a full basket of eggs.

"Pick your prize out of the box, Cuke," said the boss.

Cool Hand Cuke eyed a big, colorful sombrero. "Oooh, I'm going to wear this into town! Junior, Hot Hand, would you come too?"

"Thanks!" Junior said. "That's better than collecting a bunch of eggs and sweeping a dirty old barn!"

When they got to town, Cool Hand Cuke and the tomato hung a sign over a booth. It read: Eggs for Sale.

"Oh, I get it," Junior said. "This is how we get rich! We sell the eggs so we can go on vacation. Good idea."

The eggs sold like crazy. Their job complete, Junior, Cool Hand Cuke, and Hot Hand Tomato headed toward the city hospital.

Doctors, nurses, and patients filled the room. "What's going on?" asked Junior.

"Time for a square dance!" Cool Hand shouted.

"There are only three of us," Hot Hand whispered. "We can't make a square. How about a triangle?"

"Excellent idea!" agreed Cool Hand. Two gourds called out commands as Cuke, Hot Hand, and Junior began to do-si-do.

"Isosceles!"

"Right angle!"

"Look how happy we're making the patients," whispered Hot Hand.

When the music stopped, Hot Hand called for a break. "I'll make the tamales!"

"I'll get the drinks," Cuke offered. He headed toward the watercooler. "Sure wish we had something special to give them besides tamales."

"Do you have any peanut butter?" Junior asked.

Junior whipped up some peanut-butter shakes and served the patients.

Cool Hand Cuke got ready for his juggling act.

"Everybody loves this," the tomato whispered.
"Juggle thirty eggs today, Cuke!" yelled a pea.
"Forty!" chimed in another.
"Fifty!" called the gourds.
"Nobody can juggle fifty eggs!" shouted a nurse.

"I can!" boasted the cucumber. "That's why they call me Cool Hand Cuke." Everyone cheered as Cool Hand Cuke began to juggle. Ten . . . twenty . . . thirty . . . forty . . . and then fifty eggs!

After the party, Cuke removed his sombrero. It was filled with the money from the eggs they'd sold.

Junior's eyes popped open. "We're rich!"

"This money is for the hospital," said Cuke.
"But weren't we working to get rich?"
"What we have here is a failure to appreciate," said the tomato.
"What does that mean?" asked Junior.

"Junior, we are rich. Look at that little carrot over there. See the smile on her face? And the pea over there? See how happy he is to have a new wheelchair? We are rich in friendship and love," Cuke said.

Hot Hand showed Junior a card the patients had made. It said two simple words: THANK YOU!

"God says, 'Hands that don't want to work make you poor. But hands that work hard bring wealth to you,'" the tomato explained.

"I've got a whole summer ahead of me! Just think what I can do for others!" Junior smiled.

Just then two words floated out of the speakers: **THE END**.
Junior was swept up into the spinning letters.

After Junior landed back in the bookstore he rushed over to the café. "I'm really sorry," Junior told Laura. "I'll help you raise money for the VeggieTown Hospital. Maybe we could even provide entertainment."

"Really?" Laura asked.

"You bet! After all, hands that don't want to work make you poor. But hands that work hard bring wealth to you."

Junior began clearing the tables. Laura smiled at her friend. "What kind of entertainment did you have in mind?"

"Do you know how to juggle eggs?"

"Work as if you were not serving people but the Lord."
(Ephesians 6:7)

The Snooze Brothers

By Cindy Kenney and Doug Peterson
Illustrated by Michael Moore

BIG IDEA
BOOKS®

ZONDERkidz

ZONDERVAN.com/
AUTHORTRACKER
follow your favorite authors

Junior Asparagus and Laura Carrot were pooped!
   Babysitting wasn't easy. Li'l Pea started the morning by making mud pies on his mother's good dishes. And when Laura and Junior tried to stop him, he slung mud all over the house! After that, Junior and Laura decided they needed a break while Li'l Pea played outside.

Only one problem. Li'l Pea spotted a grasshopper. He followed it to the front of the house . . .

. . . then to the curb.

. . . and finally into the street.

Tires squealed.

Li'l Pea (and the grasshopper) hopped back in the nick of time. Whew! He was safe. But Junior and Laura were in a heap of trouble. Junior's parents were driving the car.

"Your job was to watch Li'l Pea," Junior's dad said sternly.

Junior and Laura begged for another chance.

"Not until you're able to show more responsibility." Mr. Asparagus said as he shook his head. "Being responsible means working with all your heart. You should work as if you are serving God."

Later that day, Junior and Laura visited the Treasure Trove Bookstore.

"I have just the book for you," Mr. O'Malley said. "It's somewhere in the 'Responsibility section'."

"Aye, here it is. *The Snooze Brothers.*"

"This book is about two brothers who need help," he said with a wink. "And helping them will be a true mission from God."

As Junior opened the book, four giant words floated up from inside the cover. Four simple words: Once Upon A Time...

"Wait!" Mr. O'Malley shouted. "I've got to tell you something! The Snooze Brothers are...!"

WHOOOOOOOOOOOOSH!

Too late.

The words swirled around. Junior and Laura tumbled **over**

       and over

          and over...

             and landed in a huge busy city.

Two Veggies tore down an alley, scared out of their gourds. "Help! Save us!" one of them yelled.

"What's taking the Snooze-Mobile so long?"

Junior and Laura looked at one another. "The Snooze Brothers!"

Just then a car squealed around the corner and skidded to a stop.
  Junior, Laura, and the Snooze Brothers dove into the back seat and landed in
a pile of...pillows!? The Snooze Brothers quickly snuggled in and fell asleep.

As the car sped away, the driver turned around and greeted his new passengers. "Hi! I'm Larry the Cucumber. Those two are Joliet Jammies and Snoreman Snooze. You can call them the Snooze Brothers."

"Are they in trouble?" asked Laura.

Larry pointed behind them. "Look!"

Out the rear window Junior and Laura saw cars racing after them. The drivers all had brown cases.

Junior gasped. "I bet they're hiding weapons in those cases!"

"This must be our mission from God," Laura said. "It's our responsibility to save the Snooze Brothers."

Larry grinned. "Load up the Pillow-Blaster!"
Suddenly a hatch sprung open in the roof of the car.
"Load the blaster with pillows and start firing!" shouted Larry.

Ka-pow! Whop!

Pillows smashed against the bad guys' cars. Soon the air filled with feathers.
"I want my blankie," murmured Joliet Jammies as he slept.

Things got worse. Mushrooms riding motorcycles joined the chase. They all had cases strapped to their backs.

"More pillows!" cried Junior.

Ka-pow! Zing!

Pillow after pillow zipped through the air.

"Look out!" yelled Laura.

A helicopter zoomed in.

Soon, scooters, skateboards, and pogo sticks were after them.

"Who are these guys?" asked Laura.

"Uh-oh," said Larry. "I hope you can swim."

Larry slammed on the brakes. The car skidded and spun and came to a stop inches from a lake.

The "bad guys" surrounded the Snooze-Mobile.

"We're goners!" moaned Larry.

"Not so fast!" said a little old mushroom. She jumped off her motorcycle and opened her case.

"Watch out!" Junior shouted. "She's going for her weapon!"

Ma Mushroom frowned. "Are you calling my saxophone a weapon?"

Then all of the Veggies opened their cases. They pulled out tubas, trombones, clarinets, and more.

Laura gasped. "Musical instruments! We thought you were bad guys!"

Ma Mushroom sighed. "We're musicians, not bad guys. We play the blues. The Snooze Brothers are the leaders of our band, and we're trying to get them to the church. Our show goes on in five minutes!"

"We thought the Snooze Brothers were in trouble," Laura said. "We were trying to help them."

"If you want to help, get them to the church on time," said Ma Mushroom. "Joliet Jammies and Snoreman are always running away from responsibility. The only thing they work hard at is sleeping."

Responsibility. Junior's dad used that word. It meant working with your whole heart.

"This concert will raise money to save our church!" exclaimed Ma Mushroom.

"So *this* must be our mission from God," Junior said. "Larry, can you get us to the church in five minutes?"

"No problem, boss."

"I'll lead the way!" chimed Police Officer Scooter.

Like a huge parade, the Snooze-Mobile raced behind the police car, followed by motorcycles, skateboards, and scooters.

On the way, Junior and Laura worked hard to wake the Snooze Brothers. "Sleep later," Junior said. "Right now you gotta be responsible."

The two sleepy gourds finally agreed to do their very best on stage. The crowd at the church went wild. They all sang, "Re-spon-si-bil-i-ty!, Find out what it means to me! Ohhhhhh, sock it to me, sock it to me, sock it to me..."

As the Snooze Brothers played their last song, balloons and confetti rained down. The money they earned saved the church.

Mixed in with the balloons were two large words: **THE END**.

"I guess it's time for us to go," Junior said sadly.

Joliet Jammies beamed. "Thanks for showing us how to be responsible!"

In the blink of an eye, Junior and Laura found themselves back in the bookstore.

"We did it, Mr. O'Malley! We saved the church!"

"Well done," said Mr. O'Malley. He put the "Closed" sign in the window. His hard work was over for the day.

"I can't wait to study up on babysitting," added Junior. "Do you have the books *Owies, Boo-Boos, and Other Medical Emergencies* and *101 Ways to Get Mud Off the Ceiling?* We're going to be the most responsible babysitters in town!"

"Shhh," Laura whispered. "Look."

Junior whispered, "We can tell him about it in the morning."

Laura tucked a blanket around the old potato. Junior placed a Teddy Bear next to him. They turned out the lights and slipped out the door.

Mr. O'Malley popped open one eye. He grinned, yawned, and returned to his nap.

Mission accomplished.

"Be strong, all you who put your hope in the Lord.
Never give up."

(Psalm 31:24)

Frog Wars

By Cindy Kenney and Doug Peterson
Illustrated by Michael Moore

BIG IDEA
BOOKS®

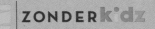

ZONDERk'dz

ZONDERVAN.com/
AUTHORTRACKER
follow your favorite authors

Junior Asparagus had been trying to learn how to play the tuba all day. But the noise coming out of it sounded like a sick water buffalo with a pail on its head. **BWOOOOOOOOMBABLUUUURRRTT-BLATT!!!** echoed through the house.

Fifteen Minutes Later...

Junior slammed his tuba on the floor.

"I quit!" he shouted as his mom rushed into the room.

"Junior, you love music. And this is the fourth instrument you've tried this month," she said.

"Ya, but I'm no good at it," he puffed.

"Perhaps it's because you're using The **Advanced** Guide to Playing Tubas on your first day. Even if God made you musically gifted, it takes perseverance before you can play well."

"Percy-fear-ants? God never gave them to me."

"Perseverance means 'keep trying; don't give up hope.'"

"Hope?" he muttered. "Nope. Don't got it."

Later That Afternoon...

Junior wandered into the Treasure Trove Bookstore.

"Do you have any books on how to play the violin?" he asked Mr. O'Malley, the Irish potato who owned the store.

Mr. O'Malley peered at Junior. "I thought you were learning to play the tuba, laddie."

"Apparently, tubas and I weren't made for each other."

Mr. O'Malley's eyes lit up. "I have the perfect book for you."

O'Malley climbed a tall ladder to find the book. "It's somewhere in the *Never-Say-Die* section, next to the Self-Help Comic Books." Finally, he found it: *Frog Wars*.

Junior opened the book and saw a beautiful palace in the middle of a desert. Workers lifted giant statues that looked like huge stone frogs.

At That Very Moment...

Four giant words floated up from the first page of the book. Four simple words: **ONCE UPON A TIME.**

The four giant words swirled around Junior, and...
WHOOOOOOOOOOOOOOOOOOOOSH!
Junior slid **down**
        down
                down.
But as he slid down the giant page, the words moved up!
They said: **A long time ago, in a land far, far away . . .**

EPISODE IV:
A REALLY, REALLY NEW HOPE
Dark Visor and his evil empire are
forcing the people of Salon to be
his slaves. He's making them build temples
to the great frog god, Ribbit. But the one
true God is rising up a hero to rescue them...

After sliding down the words, Junior crash-landed inside the *Frog Wars* book!

"Where did you come from?" asked a cucumber slave, hopping up to Junior.

"He fell from outer space," said a blueberry. "Hello, Space Boy. I'm Princess Hair-Spraya, and this is Cuke Sandwalker."

Junior stared at the cucumber's wig. Then he looked at Princess Hair-Spraya with a baffled look on his face. "You have cinnamon buns on your ears."

"Where else do you suggest I carry them?" she frowned. "I don't have hands, you know."

"Don't worry, we won't hurt you. We were captured from Salon, which is on the other side of the Big Frog Pond. We were brought here to be Dark Visor's slaves," the cucumber explained.

Just then, two other slaves peeked out from behind a frog statue. "Is it safe to come out, Master Cuke?" asked a pea dressed in gold.

"C'mon out," Cuke Sandwalker called.

The two peas cautiously approached the little asparagus. "I'm Sweet-Pea-3-Oh," said one of the peas. "This is Achoo Bless-U. We're slaves, too."

"Are you the one who's come to free our people?" asked Princess Hair-Spraya.

"I don't think so," said Junior, a little confused.

"We've been asking the one, true God to send someone who will lead us out of here. You *must* be the one!" said Cuke Sandwalker. "Follow us, Space Boy."

Junior stayed close behind as Cuke and his friends rushed through the palace and into the throne room.

The king, a zucchini named Dark Visor, sat on a great frog throne. His visor made his breathing sound funny.

"He hates the sunlight," whispered Achoo Bless-U.

"What's with all the frogs?" Junior asked.

"Dark Visor believes in a frog god called Ribbit," Princess Hair-Spraya told him. "He doesn't believe the true God will send someone to help us."

"So go ahead and tell him," nudged Cuke.

"Tell him what?" asked Junior.

"Tell him to let God's people go free!"

Trembling With Fear...

Junior moved toward the king.

"What do you want?" Dark Visor bellowed after lifting his visor.

"Let the people of Salon go free," Junior squeaked.

"NO!" thundered the king so loudly it caused his visor to slam shut.

"Okay, I gave it a shot," Junior shrugged and turned to leave.

"Wait!" said Cuke Sandwalker. "You hardly tried at all!"

"Trying isn't really my thing," Junior added as he ran for the door.

At That Very Moment...

. . . a guy named Mo stormed into the room carrying a walking stick. The big round tomato was on a mission.

"Stick with me," Mo told Junior. "We won't give up until Dark Visor gives in." Mo turned to the king and spoke. "My name is Mo! And God wants you to let his people go!"

But Dark Visor only snarled at him with a heavy breath.

"**Whmmmimmtwyouttodsiiiiiiii**."

"Huh?" everyone gasped.

"Lift your visor, and try it again," suggested Sweet-Pea-3-Oh.

The king flung his head back to open the visor and roared, "When I'm through with you, you will all turn to the dark side!"

Dark Visor would not let the slaves go free. But did Mo give up? Nope! He had hope and would not give up, because he put his faith in the Lord.

Mo warned Dark Visor that God would not be pleased, but the big zucchini didn't care. So Mo threatened to turn all the water in the kingdom to juice, and soon purple liquid bubbled from every drinking fountain in the city.

"This guy's really good," Cuke Sandwalker whispered to Junior.

Day After Day After Day...

Mo threatened the king with God's anger, but the king refused to let the people go. Junior just wanted to quit and go home.

But Mo encouraged him to stay. "God wants us to have faith in him. That means doing our best and *not* giving up," he told Junior. Then Mo shouted, "My name is Mo! And God wants you to let his people go!"

"No way, Jose," Dark Visor replied as he sipped his juice.

So the tomato warned the king that God would send plagues on the land. And plagues were scary things like...

...days and days of doing the Hokey Pokey.

...swarms of dust bunnies.

...a drought of pizza and ice cream.

...and the invasion of FROGS!

Even though the king worshiped the frog Ribbit, unwanted, *real* frogs turned up everywhere! The king found them in his cereal bowl. In his pajamas. Even on his throne! But Dark Visor would not let God's people go free.

Many Days Later...

"Isn't it time to give up?" asked Cuke Sandwalker.

"What do you think, Junior?" Mo asked.

Junior thought about it. *God wants us to put our hope in him and keep trying!*

"Anything else we can try?" Junior asked.

Mo smiled, and they prayed to God for help.

Then God sent a deep darkness to fall upon the land.

"Is this what you meant when you talked about turning to the dark side?"
Achoo Bless-U teased the king.

Finally...

...an amazing thing happened. Dark Visor heard that familiar voice... "My name is Mo! And God wants you to let his people go!"

"I can't see anything in the dark!" he groaned as he flipped his visor up just as he was about to sit on a frog. "Ribbit has turned against me in my time of need.

"Alright! Let the slaves go free, and take these frogs with you!" the king shouted.

The clouds began to part as the slaves marched out of the land. Junior rode in a wagon with his new friends, except there was no room for Cuke Sandwalker.

"Use the horse, Cuke!" said the princess.

"Good thinking," smiled the cucumber.

But Before the Slaves Could Get Away...

Dark Visor slammed down the lid of his visor and sent his army to chase after the slaves.

"**IchkabildGoafrtthslvsfslnan!**"

"Huh?"

He flipped his visor back open and shouted, "I changed my mind! Go after the slaves from Salon!"

The Empire struck back!

The slaves were trapped in front of the Big Frog Pond with no way to get across. In front of the slaves was the treacherous pond muck. The king's army was quickly approaching them. The people from Salon were afraid.

Junior was scared, too. But did he give up? Nope! He had hope! He saw how God continued to watch over the people again and again. He knew they had to trust God in a mighty way.

"Don't give up!" Junior shouted.

Then Mo called out: "You will see how the Lord will save you!"

Suddenly...

The lily pads in the pond came together and turned to stone while the waters parted to each side. God created a pathway so the slaves could get to the other side.

But Dark Visor's army was right behind them.

Did Junior and Mo give up?

Nope! They had hope!

As the Sun Began To Rise...

The slaves arrived on the other side of the pond, and the lily pads returned to normal. The pond filled with water and muck. The soldiers sank into tons of mud and water, and clamored to shore.

"It's not easy being mean," said the king, pulling himself out of the muck.

"Ribbit," said a frog behind him.

With the army defeated, the slaves cheered on the opposite shore.

And Then It Happened...

Two words suddenly popped out of the sand...along with several frogs. Two simple words: **THE END.**

"Thanks for not giving up, Junior!" said Mo.

"Thanks for teaching me to never give up!" replied Junior.

"Goodbye, Space Boy!" called Princess Hair-Spraya.

"Be strong and never lose hope," added Cuke Sandwalker. "May the Lord be with you."

The two giant words swirled around Junior like a desert whirlwind. The next thing Junior knew, he was back in the Treasure Trove Bookstore, shaking sand from his hat.

In the Store...

Mr. O'Malley shuffled out of the back room when he heard the bell above the door jingle.

Junior told Mr. O'Malley all about his adventure. Dark Visor. The frogs. Mo.

"Aye, but what did you learn?" asked Mr. O'Malley.

"That God wants us to have hope in him. And that we shouldn't give up, even when things get difficult," he said. "By the way, do you have The **Beginner's** Guide to Playing Tubas?"

"I sure do, laddie!" Mr. O'Malley chuckled. "Let it be my gift to you."

"Thanks!" Junior beamed as he hopped out of the store.

Then, Mr. O'Malley said to himself, New hope you have. Happy that makes me.

Want to read a real story about having hope in the Lord?
Read the story of Moses in Exodus, Chapters 1 to 15, in the Bible.

"We hope for what we don't have yet.
So we are patient as we wait for it."

(Romans 8:25)

Ben Hurry

By Doug Peterson
Illustrated by Michael Moore

bigidea.com

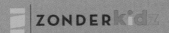

ZONDERVAN.com/
AUTHORTRACKER
follow your favorite authors

"Are we there yet?" asked Junior and Laura.
One minute later, they asked again, "Are we there yet?"
Thirty seconds later . . .
"ARE WE—"

"No, we're not there yet," grumbled Bob the Tomato.

"Kids, you'll be much happier if you learn to wait," added Mr. Asparagus. "Waiting means being patient. And patience is a gift from God."

But Junior and Laura didn't think they could wait another millisecond to get to the new Lobster-Land Theme Park. They felt like they were going to explode.

Suddenly, Bob stopped the car.

"Traffic," he growled. "Everyone in VeggieTown must be going to Lobster-Land today."

He was right. Cars on the road stretched for miles. It was going to take forever to get there. Even Dad Asparagus was getting impatient.

"That's it! I'm not waiting another second!" Bob said. He turned quickly onto a side road. "I know a shortcut."

Junior and Laura cheered as their car began to move again. But the shortcut led them onto a bumpy, narrow road. Even worse, they got stuck behind a slow truck carrying a load to the Nails 'R' Us hardware store.

"Are we there yet?" asked Junior and Laura.

Thump!

The truck in front of them hit a big bump, spilling nails all over the road.

"Look out!"

Pop! Pow!

Sssssss. Their front tires were flatter than squished pancakes.

The next day Junior and Laura went to the Treasure Trove Bookstore. "I can't believe we didn't make it to Lobster-Land," Junior said.

"We'll have to wait forever to go again," muttered Laura.

"Wait right here," said Mr. O'Malley, the owner of the store. "I've got the perfect book for you."

The old potato shuffled to the bookshelf like a tired turtle. "I think the book is in the 'Where's the Fire?' section. Here it is, right next to the edible cookbooks."

Junior and Laura opened the book to a picture of a huge Roman ship.
Soldiers in gleaming armor stood on the deck.

As they looked at the page, four giant words floated up from the book. Four simple words: Once Upon A Time.

The words swirled around Junior and Laura. They whirled and twirled and . . .

WHOOOOOOOOOOOSH!

Junior and Laura tumbled **down**
          down
               down.

Whomp!

Junior and Laura landed on the deck of the ship they had seen in the book. A second later they were being pushed along by a little Roman pea named Ben Hurry. "Hurry up, hurry up! We don't have all day. Get rowing!"

"Move, move, move!" yelled another pea named Maximus Hurrius, or Max, for short. "We've got to get to Rome now!"

"What's going on?" Junior asked as the peas dragged him and Laura
below deck.

"No time to talk!" barked Ben Hurry.

Below deck were rows and rows of Veggies, pulling on huge wooden oars.

"We're missing two rowers!" exclaimed Ben. "Take a seat! Hurry!"

"There's not a moment to lose," added Max as he pushed Laura onto a bench.

"What's the rush?" Laura snapped.

"We're going to Rome to see the Monster Chariot Show!" shouted Ben.

"Wait until you see those monster chariots drive over rows of little chariots!" yelled Max. "It's the coolest thing. But we gotta get there as fast as possible!"

Junior and Laura rowed like crazy.

A Roman cucumber sat in front of the rowers and beat on a drum. The faster the drum beat, the faster everyone had to row.

"Are we there yet?" asked Ben Hurry.

"No! Increase to Impatient Speed!" yelled Max.

"Impatient Speed!" repeated the drummer, and he began to drum even faster.

The rowers picked up speed.

"Are we there yet?" asked Ben.

"No!" shouted Max. "Increase to Freaky-Fast Speed!"

"Freaky-Fast Speed!" repeated the drummer. Then the cucumber began to drum so fast that sparks flew. The rowers rowed so fast that some of the oars snapped.

"This is crazy!" Junior gasped, trying to keep up.

But Ben didn't care. He started to sing: "Row, row, row the boat, quickly down the stream! Hurry, hurry, hurry, hurry! Or I'm going to scream!" "Faster!" yelled Max. "It's taking us forever to get to Rome!"

Up ahead, Junior spotted hundreds of ships headed toward Rome.
"It's a traffic jam. We've got to slow down!" shouted Junior.
"No way!" boomed Ben. "Increase to Warped Speed!"
"Warped Speed!" yelled the cucumber. He drummed faster than the speed of light.
"We can't keep up!" Laura gasped.
Their ship zipped across the water, headed straight for the long line of boats.

"We're going to ram another ship!" shouted one of the rowers.
"We've got to stop!"
"Nothing doing!" yelled Max.
"Move into the passing lane!" Ben ordered. "Hurry! Hurry! Hurry!"
But it was too late. They rammed into another ship.

Cra-a-ack!

Wood splintered. Water gushed in through a hole in the front of their boat.

"Keep rowing!" cried Ben.

"Hurry!"

Water came up to the drummer's nose. "Are we there yet?" he gurgled.

Within minutes, the ship sank. Some of the ship's crew swam to shore. Everyone else climbed onto floating chunks of wood. Junior and Laura wound up on the same piece of wood as Max, Ben, and the drummer.

"You really need to learn how to wait," Junior told Ben. "I should know. I have a hard time waiting for things too. But patience is a gift from God."

"It would have made me so happy to get to Rome as fast as I could," said Ben.

"When you can't wait, you usually end up unhappy," said Laura.

The drummer hit his soggy drum. "I'm definitely unhappy," he muttered.

Later that day, Junior, Laura, the drummer, and the two peas finally reached Rome. But they missed the Monster Chariot Show.

"We can still make the Brutus 500 chariot race," said the drummer.

"We'll have to hurry," said Max.

"No need to hurry," Ben said. "Patience is a gift from God, you know."

They missed the beginning of the chariot race, but they still had a great time. When the race was over, two large words appeared on the side of the winning chariot: **THE END**.

"It's time for us to leave," said Junior sadly.

"So soon?" said Ben.

"Will you come back and visit?" asked Max.

"Maybe some day," said Laura.

"We'll be waiting."

In a flash, Junior and Laura found themselves back in the Treasure Trove Bookstore.

"Welcome home!" shouted Mr. O'Malley. "I want to hear all about your adventure. But first, you might like to see these. I've got tickets to Lobster-Land, and I'm taking both of you!" he announced.

Junior and Laura couldn't believe their ears. "When are we going? When? When? When?!"

"Well, that's the catch," said Mr. O'Malley. "We can't go for two weeks."
The smiles suddenly vanished from Junior's and Laura's faces. "Oh."
But ever so slowly, the grins returned.
"We can wait!" Laura declared.
"That's the spirit!" said Mr. O'Malley. "After all, Rome wasn't built in a day. It took patience."

"Lobster-Land, here we come!" said Junior.

Were they there yet?
No, they weren't. But that was okay. They were happy to wait.

"Blessed are those who make peace.
They will be called sons of God."

(Matthew 5:9)

West Slide Story

By Doug Peterson
Illustrated by Michael Moore

BIG IDEA
BOOKS®

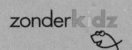
zonderkidz

ZONDERVAN.COM/
AUTHORTRACKER

"No boys allowed," said Megan Radish. "Besides, we were here first."

"We called 'dibs,'" said Lenny Carrot. "So the boys get the jungle gym today!"
"We called 'double dibs'!" answered Megan. "So the girls get to play here all week!"
"You can't call double dibs!"
"Can too!"
"Cannot!"
"Can . . . !"
It was just another day on the VeggieTown playground.

The giant new jungle gym had monkey bars and slides and climbing tubes.
"It's amazing," the girls said. "It's our turn to use it."
"No, it's awesome," argued the boys. "And it's our turn to use it."

"It's big enough for everyone," Laura Carrot whispered to Junior Asparagus. Junior agreed. But they were afraid to point this out. Laura thought the girls would get mad. Junior feared the boys would say he was siding with the girls.

So they did nothing, and the arguing went on.

"Can!"

"Can't!"

"Can!"

Later that day, Junior and Laura went to the Treasure Trove Bookstore to get away from the bickering on the playground.

"The playground is no fun anymore," Laura complained as she smacked her bubblegum.

"I wish we could stop the fighting," said Junior.

"But you *can* do something," said Mr. O'Malley, owner of the bookstore. "All of God's children can be peacemakers. When you make peace, everyone wins. I've got just the book to prove it."

The old Irish potato hopped onto a rolling book cart and coasted down a long aisle. "You'll love this book. It's somewhere in the 'Give Peas a Chance' section, not far from my copy of *War and Peas*."

Mr. O'Malley tossed Junior a book called *West Slide Story*. Junior opened it to a picture of two groups of kids facing each other on a playground. Suddenly, four giant words floated up from the book. Four simple words: Once Upon A Time . . .

The words swirled around Junior and Laura. They whirled and twirled and . . .

WHOOOOOOOOOOOOSH!

Junior and Laura tumbled **down**

down

down.

Clunk!

They landed smack-dab on a giant slide. They zipped down the twisting slide like a pair of rockets and landed right between two groups of kids.

A cucumber named Hairbrush yanked Junior into his group and said, "You're with us, not them, Daddy-O." The kids in the cucumber's group wore black leather jackets and looked like they had smeared grease in their hair. They were the "Greaseballs".

Laura started to follow Junior. A broccoli girl named Beehive stopped her.
"Where ya goin', sister?" said Beehive. She smacked her gum.
"I'm following my . . . uh . . . friend," squeaked Laura.

Beehive blew a huge bubble. "But you're chewing gum, so you're with us, not them. We're the Gumballs, and we don't hang out with Greaseballs."

"Oh . . . right." Laura stared at the ground and backed away.

All at once, the two groups started circling each other. They made the sound of fingers snapping—which seemed strange since none of them had fingers.

Snap! Snap! Snap! Snap!

"What's going on?" Junior asked Hairbrush.

"We're going to decide once and for all who gets to use the big slide here at West Slide Park," said Hairbrush. "Will it be the Greaseballs or the Gumballs?"

Junior glanced around. The slide looked plenty big enough for everyone. But Junior kept quiet.

Snap! Snap! Snap! Snap!

"So, how are you going to decide?" Junior asked.

"That's easy," said a gourd called Rebel Without a Comb. "We're going to hoop for it."

With that, everyone pulled out a hula hoop. They twirled the hoops around and around and around.

The Gumballs and Greaseballs gave Junior and Laura hoops too. "Twirl 'em," they said.

"Why?" Laura asked.

"This is a battle to the finish," Beehive answered. "Whoever keeps their hula hoop going the longest wins. If a Gumball wins, we get the slide. If a Greaseball wins, they get the slide."

But there was something the West Slide Park kids didn't know. Junior and Laura were champion hula-hoopers.

Ten minutes went by. Seven kids dropped out. But Junior and Laura kept going strong.

"Go, man, go!"

"Play it cool, cat!"

As time went on, the kids gave up, one by one. Finally, there were only two—Junior and Laura.

All of the kids formed a circle around them. Neither one showed any sign of tiring.

Beehive and her friends popped bubblegum in Junior's face. That didn't stop Junior. Hairbrush and his buddies squirted greasy hair stuff on the ground around Laura. But she didn't fall—or stop.

Junior and Laura thought the two groups should forget the contest and play together in peace. But they were too afraid to say anything.

One hour later, it seemed as if the contest would never end.
Both sides glared at each other. Junior and Laura didn't know what to do.

Then Junior remembered Mr. O'Malley's words: "All of God's children can be peacemakers."

Junior and Laura had to take action.

But did they have the courage?

Then the most incredible thing happened.
They stopped hula-hooping.
In stunned silence, everyone watched as Junior's and Laura's hula hoops
came to a stop and hit the ground—at the exact same moment.

"Who won?" asked a baffled Rebel.

"Everyone wins!" exclaimed Junior.

"It's a tie!" said Laura. "And that means all of the kids get to use the slide."

"But . . . but . . . ," sputtered Hairbrush.

Beehive was so shocked, her bubblegum popped right in her own face.

"Let's go, Daddy-Os," Junior said. "We all slide!"

After a moment of shock, all the kids swarmed the giant slide. And to their amazement, they found that it was more fun to make peace than make trouble.

"Just call me Peacemaker," Hairbrush said. "That's my new nickname."

The kids ended the day with a sock-hop—a game in which they hopped over socks to the sound of music. And as they did, two giant words came slipping down the slide: **THE END**.

"It's time to go," said Laura sadly.

"Peace, sister," said Beehive with a smile.

With a final farewell, Junior and Laura slid back home and found themselves in the Treasure Trove Bookstore.

Mr. O'Malley was doing the hula hoop to the sound of Elvis music. What a scary sight.

"Did everything work out in *West Slide Story*?" asked the old potato.

"You bet," said Junior.

"And you were right," added Laura. "When you make peace, everyone wins."

"God was right," declared Mr. O'Malley. "Come on! Grab a hula hoop!"

Suddenly, Mr. O'Malley began to sing . . . off-key: "Tonight! Tonight! There won't be any fight. Tonight there will be peace all around!"

"Uh—we gotta get going," said Junior as he and Laura slipped out the door.

Junior and Laura headed straight for the VeggieTown playground. There they made peace between the girls and boys.

"It's been a long, crazy day," Laura said.

Junior yawned. "I think we need a little peas and quiet."